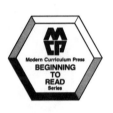

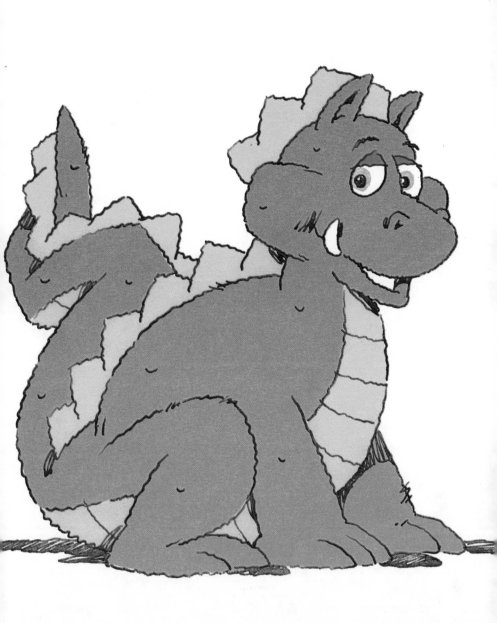

A Friend for Dear Dragon

Margaret Hillert

Illustrated by David Helton

MODERN CURRICULUM PRESS
Cleveland • Toronto

© **1985 MODERN CURRICULUM PRESS, INC.**
13900 Prospect Road, Cleveland, Ohio 44136.

All rights reserved. Printed in the United States of America.

Softcover edition published simultaneously in Canada by
Globe/Modern Curriculum Press, Toronto.

Library of Congress Cataloging in Publication Data

Hillert, Margaret.
  A friend for dear dragon.

  Summary: A boy and his pet dragon make friends with
their new neighbors, a girl and her unicorn.
  (1. Friendship — Fiction.   2. Dragons — Fiction)
I. Helton, David, ill.   II. Title.
PZ7.H558Fr   1984   (E)   83-22074

ISBN 0-8136-5636-2   Paperback
ISBN 0-8136-5136-0   Hardbound

        6 7 8 9 10   02 01 00 99 98 97

Come here.

Come here.

I want you to see something.

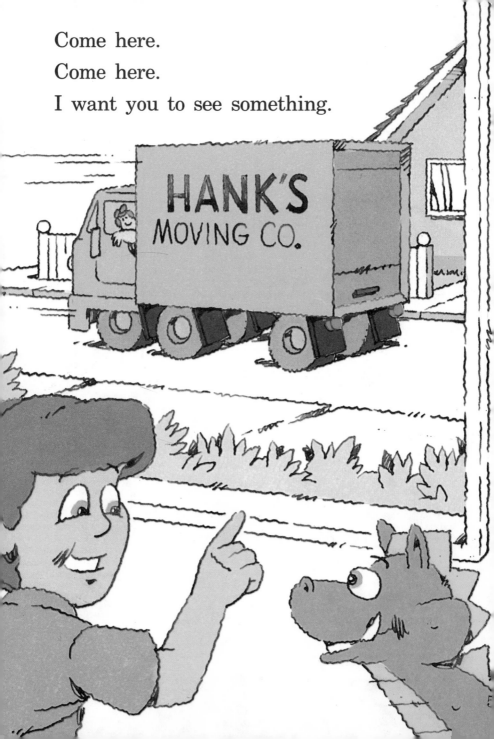

Oh, oh.
Look at that.
Do you see what I see?

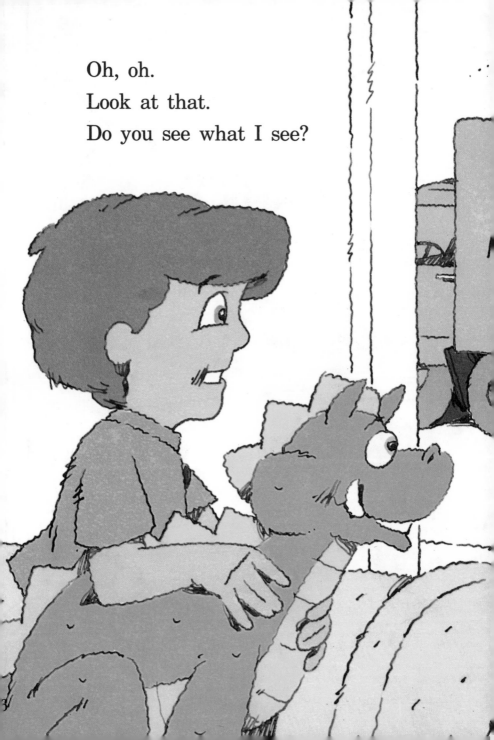

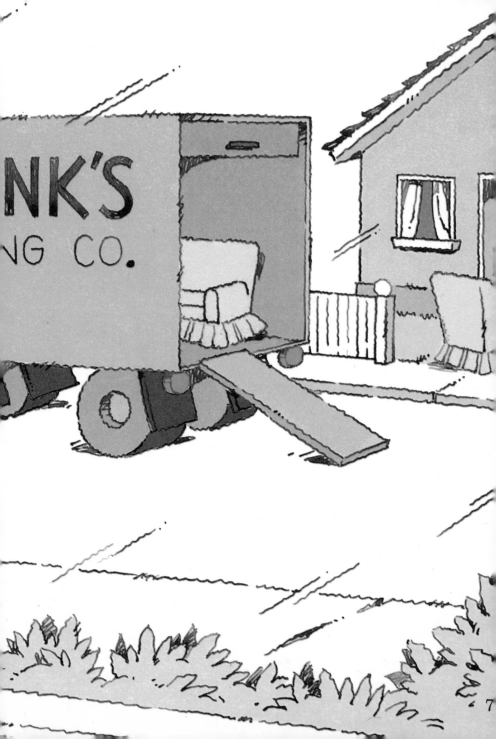

Look at that man.
How big he is!
What will he do?

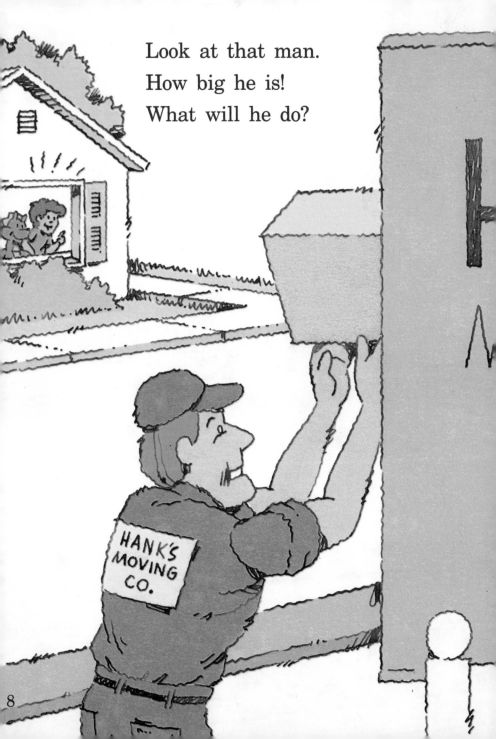

HANK'S
MOVING
CO.

Oh, now I see.
Here he comes with
something for that house.

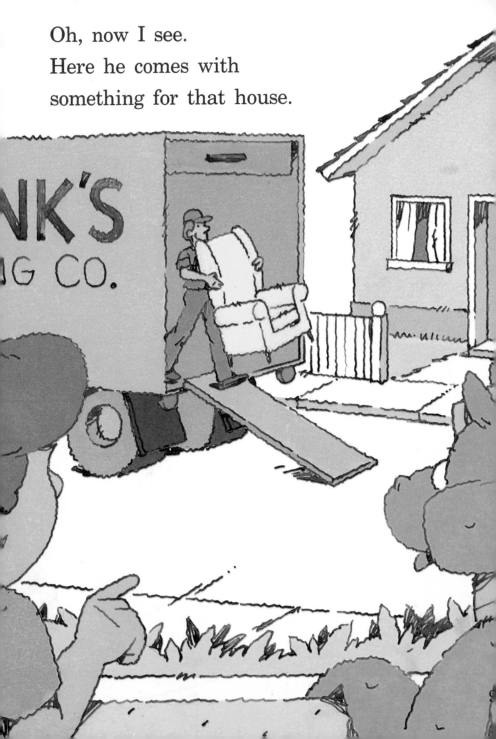

Here comes a car.
Who is in it?
Can you see who is in it?

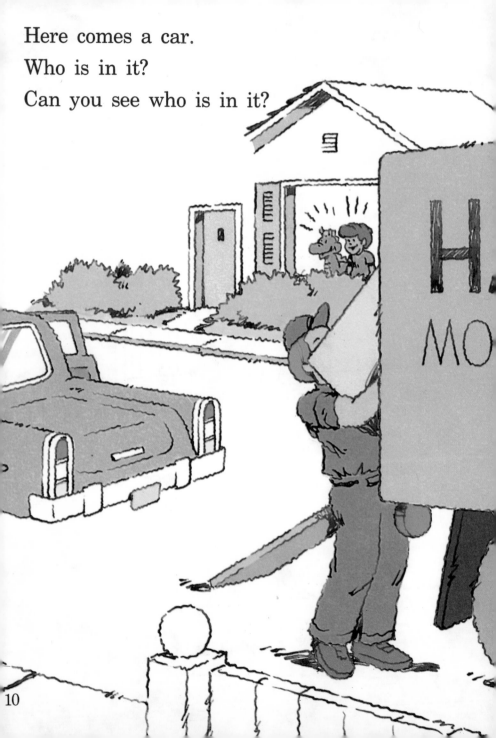

Oh, oh.
It looks like a
friend for me.
Good, good.

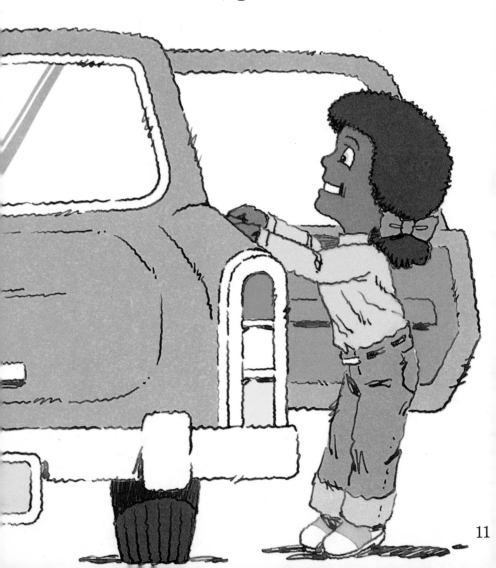

And look, look.
A friend for you, too.
What a pretty little one.

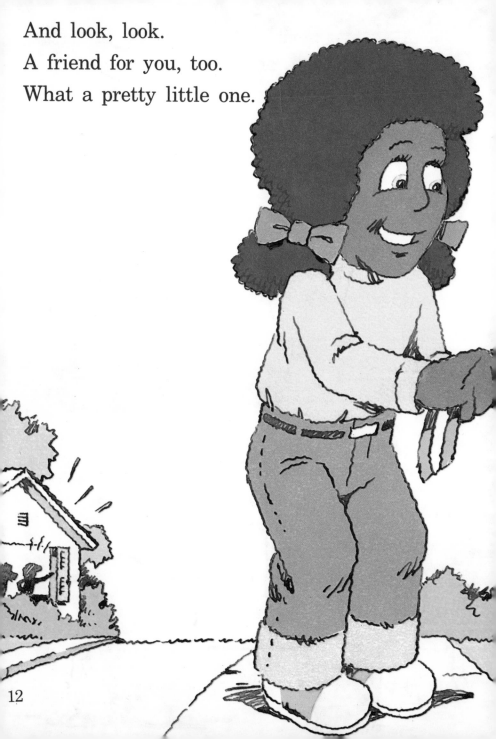

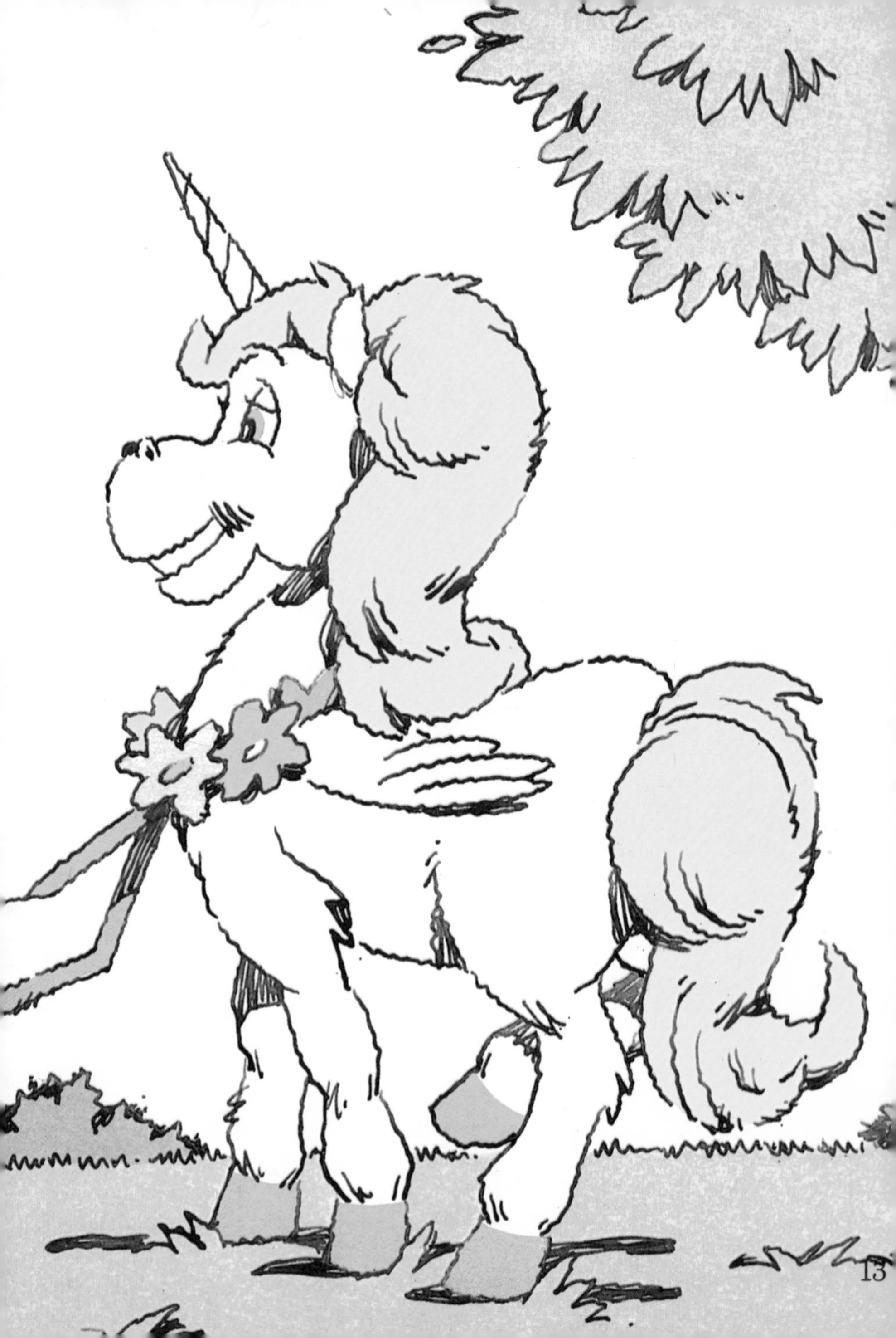

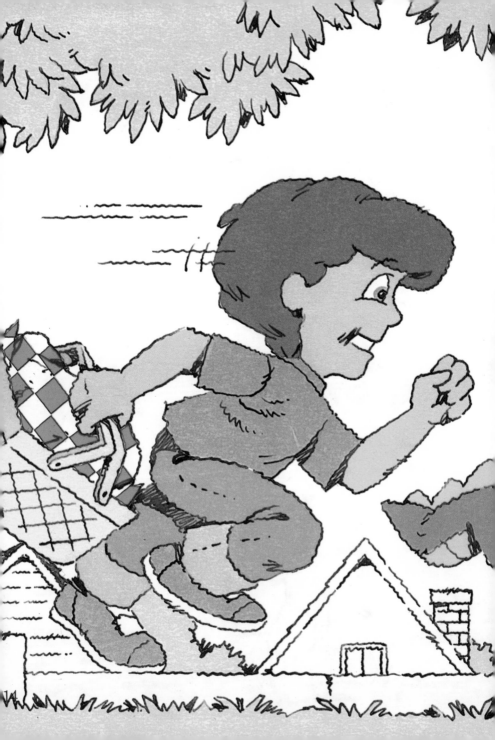

Come on.
Come on.
Here we go.
Out, out, out.

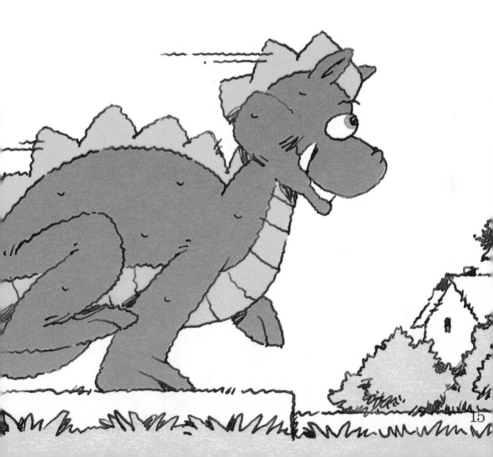

We are happy to see you.
You look like friends for us.
That is good.
We can play and have fun.

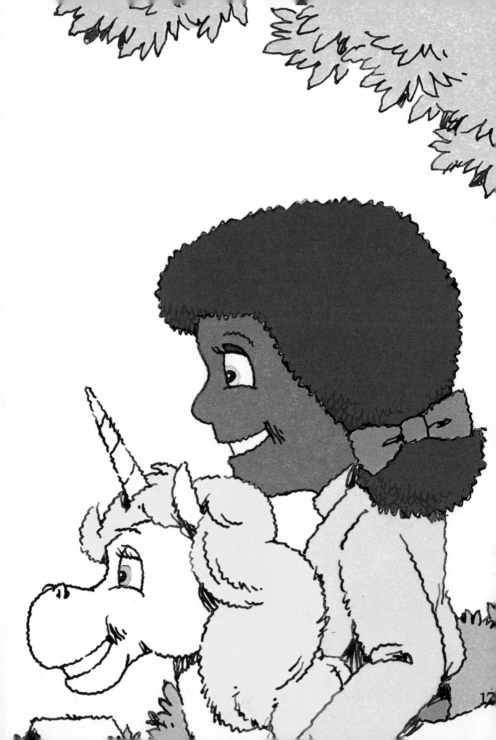

17

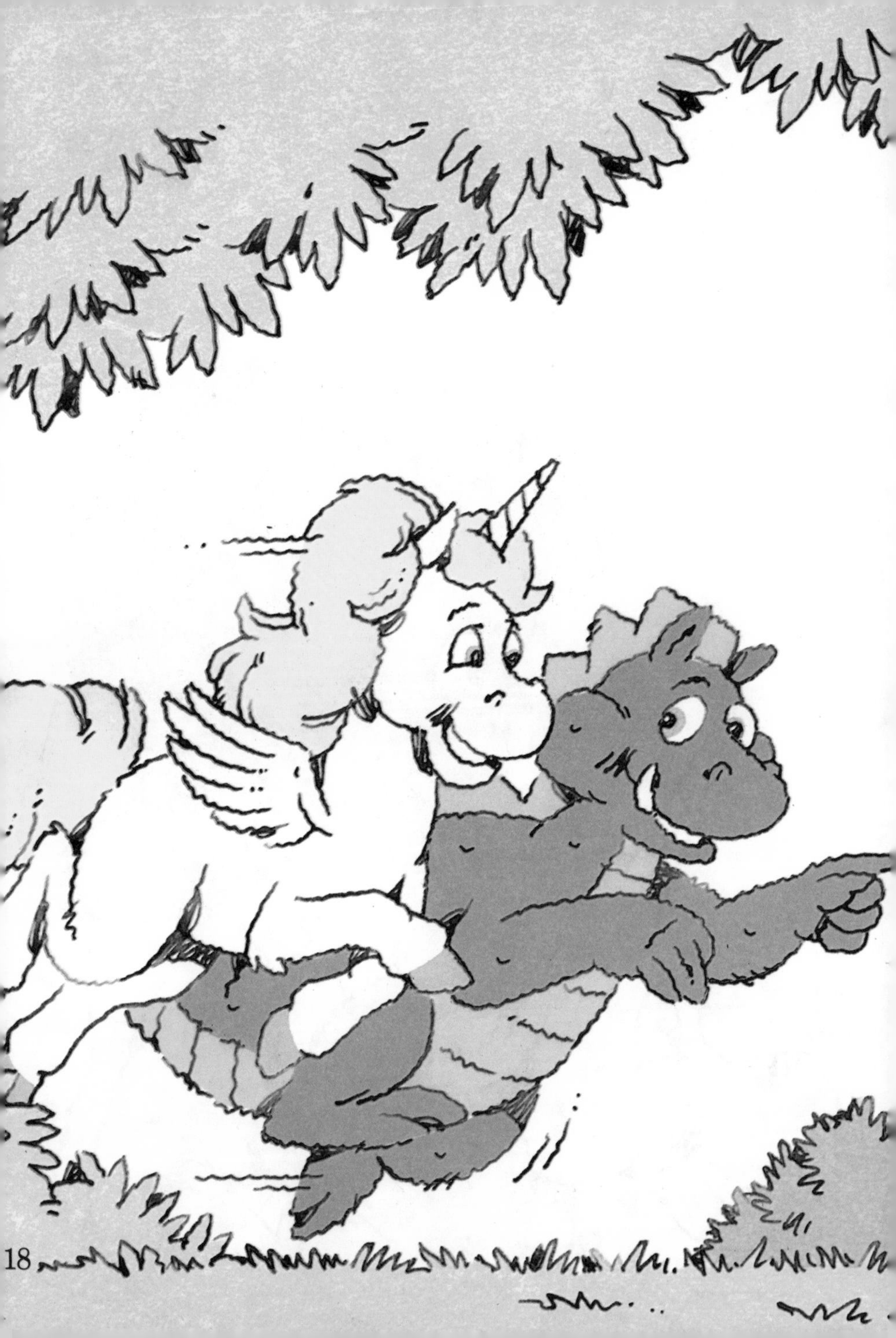

Come on.

Run, run, run.

What fun this is!

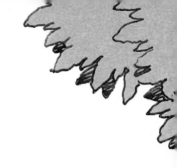
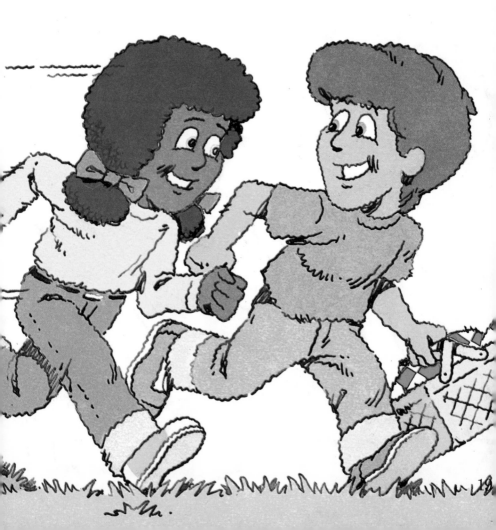

Now, look at this.
See what we two can do.
We like to play like this.

See, see.

He is good at this.

Look what he can do.

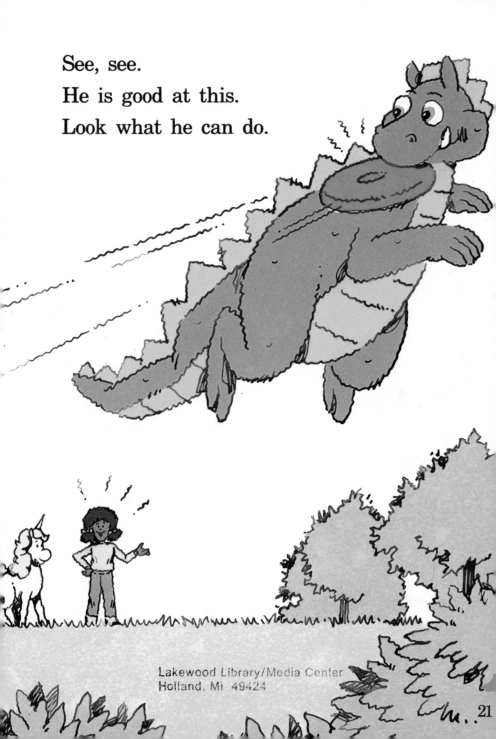

21

Yes, yes.

I see.

I see.

But we can do a good thing, too.

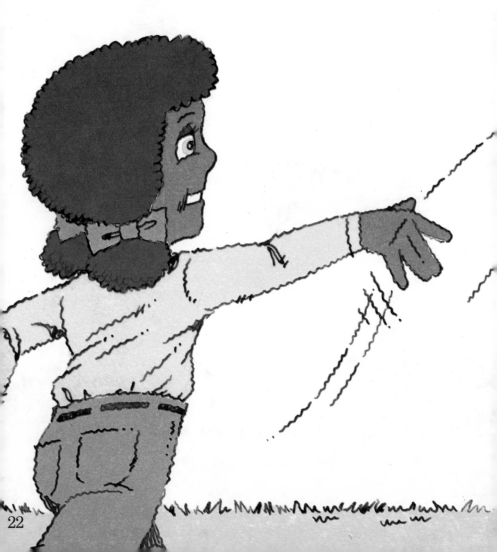

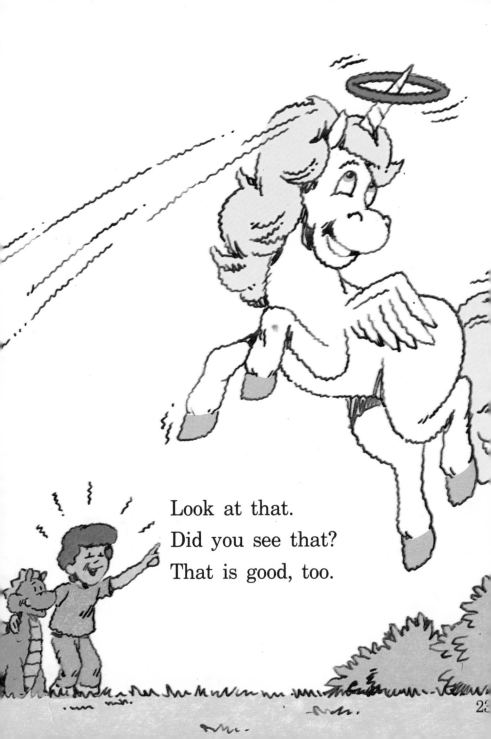

Look at that.
Did you see that?
That is good, too.

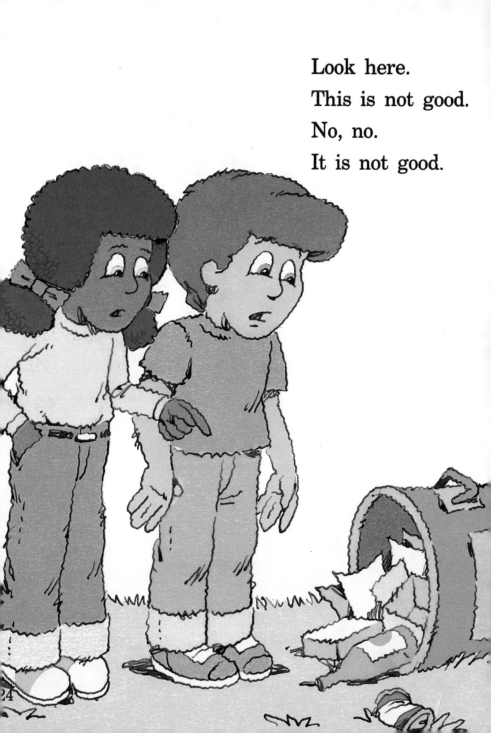

Look here.
This is not good.
No, no.
It is not good.

We two can help.
Get to work.
We can do this and this.
It will go in here.

Oh, my.

You are a big help, too.

You can get it for us.

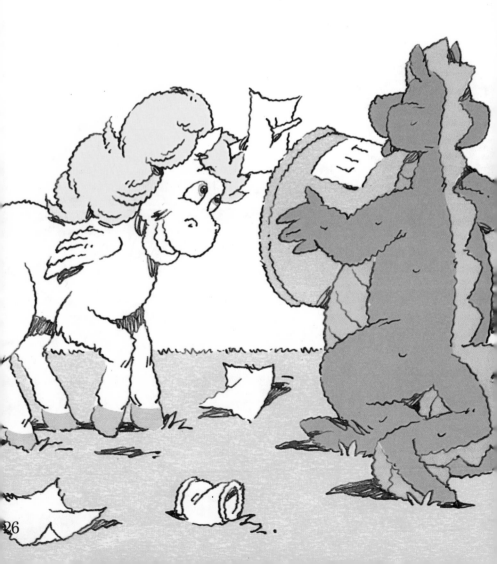

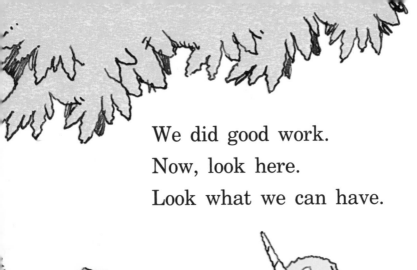

We did good work.
Now, look here.
Look what we can have.

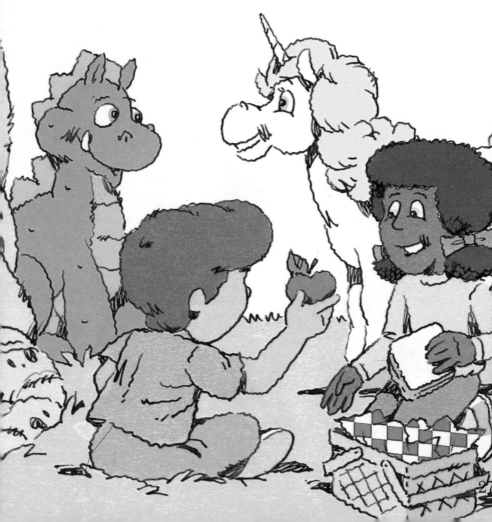

Oh, how good this is.
We like to eat this.
We are happy.

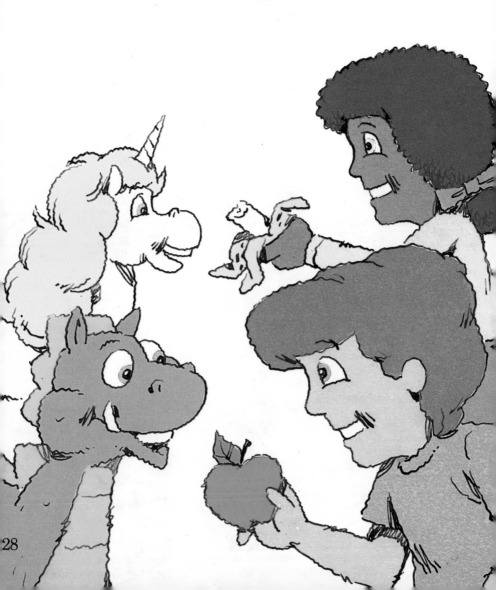

We are happy to have friends.
But we have to go home now.

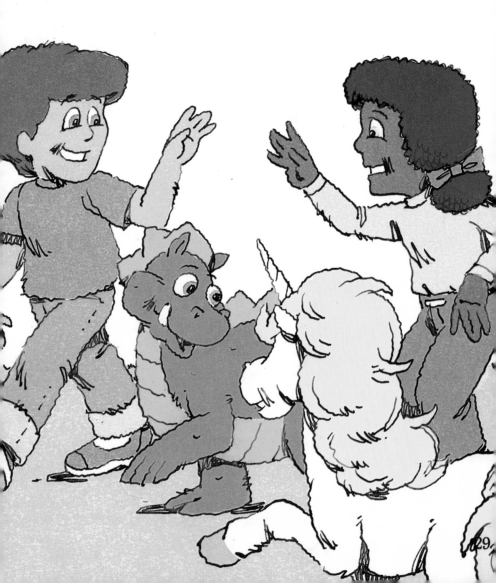

Here you are with me.
And here I am with you.
Oh, it is good to have
friends, dear dragon.

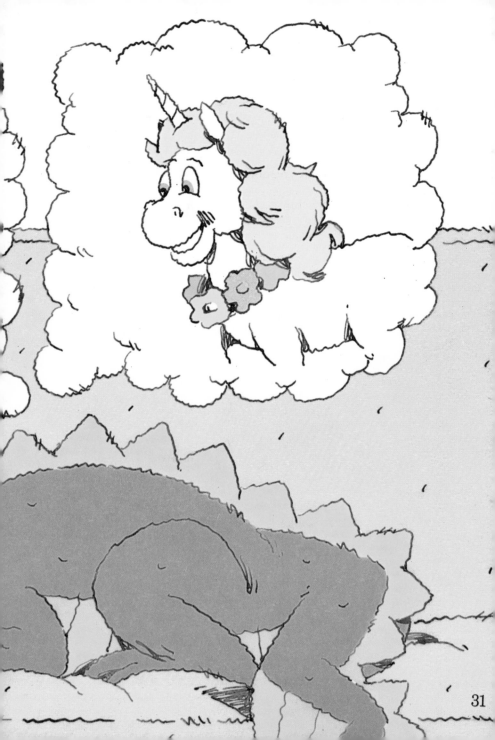

Margaret Hillert, author and poet, has written many books for young readers. She is a former first-grade teacher and lives in Birmingham, Michigan.

A Friend for Dear Dragon uses the 67 words listed below.

a	fun	look	that
am			thing
and	get	man	this
are	go	me	to
at	good	my	too
			two
big	happy	no	
but	have	not	us
	he	now	
can	help		want
car	here	oh	we
come	home	on	what
	house	one	who
dear	how	out	will
did			with
do	I	play	work
dragon	in	pretty	
	is		yes
eat	it	run	you
for	like	see	
friend	little	something	

DATE DUE

FOLLETT